SKYLANDERS UNIVERSE

MAGIC & TECH

 BOOK OF ELEMENTS

SUNBIRD
PENGUIN

Published by Ladybird Books Ltd 2012
A Penguin Company
Penguin Books Ltd, 80 Strand, London, WC2R 0RL, UK
Penguin Group (USA) Inc., 375 Hudson Street, New York 10014, USA
Penguin Books Australia Ltd, 707 Collins Street, Melbourne, Victoria 3008,
Australia (A division of Pearson Australia Group Pty Ltd)
Canada, India, New Zealand, South Africa

Written and designed by Shubrook Bros. Creative
Sunbird is a trademark of Ladybird Books Ltd

www.ladybird.com

ISBN: 978-1-40939-122-7
006
Printed in China

MAGIC & TECH

BOOK OF ELEMENTS

CONTENTS

MAGIC

TECH

WELCOME!
FROM FLYNN AND HUGO

Hey there! Welcome to my book all about Magic and Tech. That's right - if you wanna find out all about the history and secrets of these two Elements, you've come to the right super-awesome guy! I've got all the inside scoop, so get ready for some pretty awesome stuff.

FEW ELEMENTS RIVAL THE COMBINED POWER OF MAGIC AND TECH.

Pay little attention to Flynn. He didn't write this book; I did. Or most of it, anyway. After all, he knows little about the history of Skylands. He can tell a captivating story, for sure, but there's little evidence to back up his claims. For my part, I have endeavoured to relay as many facts as I can about these two wonderful and essential Elements.

WHERE DOES MAGIC COME FROM?

Magic is the force that binds all of Skylands together. It flows through everything from the animals to the trees. But where did it come from and who put it there? Well . . . er . . . no-one really knows. The history of Magic in our realm can be traced right back to before the Ancient Arkeyans. They discovered that a substance called Quicksilver was the very essence of all magical being. They harnessed the power of Magic and combined it with technology to create huge and powerful weapons of war. Scary stuff!

IN SKYLANDS, EVEN THE SHEEP ARE MAGIC! (NOT TO MENTION TERRIFYING)

MAGIC CAN BE FOUND ALL ACROSS SKYLANDS.

With these colossal weapons, they ruled our world with an unyeilding power – that is, until their rule came to a mysterious end 10,000 years ago.

THE WEAPON MASTERS

A mysterious statue had long rested in the middle of the sea in the Ruins. For thousands of years the residents of Skylands wondered what this statue was and why it was there. Then, after thousands of years of silence, it woke up and spoke in a deep, resonating voice. And I thought Flynn liked to sleep!

THE ARKEYAN WEAPON MASTER STOOD MOTIONLESS FOR 10,000 YEARS!

AFTER ALL THAT TIME AS A STATUE, THE WEAPON MASTER HAD QUITE A LOT TO CHAT ABOUT!

It was soon found that the ancient statue held a wealth of knowledge about the Arkeyans and their harnessing of Magic. This was information that we thought had been lost forever! Or at least carelessly mis-placed.

THE ETERNAL SOURCE OF MAGIC

The Eternal Source of Magic was the birthplace of all creations. Its power is so great that it cannot be contained, even by Skylands' greatest civilisation, the Arkeyans. The Weapon Masters stored the Magic Source in their Armoury where it was guarded for one purpose - to prevent future generations from discovering their secrets. And what was their biggest secret of all? Nobody knows - it's a secret! Shhhh!

THE SOURCE LAY HIDDEN IN THE ARKEYAN ARMOURY.

QUICKSILVER

Quicksilver is the energy that flows through all things magic (even the sheep!). It is an ancient oil that is essential to Magic within the Core of Light and must be used to bind every other element together. Quicksilver is guarded deep in an Arkeyan Vault. It's almost as if they didn't want anyone to know of its existence!

THE GLISTENING, MAGICAL OIL KNOWN AS QUICKSILVER.

SPREAD OF THE DARKNESS

The immense spread of the Darkness is generally considered to be Kaos' fault. In fact, it definitely was his fault. He sent his minions to destroy the Core of Light, but his evil-doers were confronted by Eon's Skylanders. In the ensuing battle, the Skylanders used all their magic to fend off his nasties. Kaos was used to losing (it's what he does best), but this time he had the Darkness on his side. Kaos won the battle, and Skylands would never be the same again. Oh dear.

MAGIC BEGINS!

MAGIC DESTROYED?

Kaos summoned a massive khydra to destroy the Core of Light, causing a huge explosion (weirdly, those awful sheep all managed to survive!). This colossal bang obliterated everything in its path, including Master Eon. Luckily, Magic is strong with the great Portal Master and he survived in spirit form (which, thankfully, is less spooky than it sounds).

FROZEN IN TIME

The Skylanders were not destroyed by the explosion of the Core of Light. By the power of Magic, they were banished in balls of light and jettisoned from Skylands into space. As they hurtled through the unknown, they shrank and froze in time before landing on a strange, smelly world filled with horrifying creatures - Earth! There they found new Portal Masters to aid their cause.

SPYRO

FACTFILE

- Comes from a land of which few have heard (me included)
- Mentioned prominently in the ancient scrolls
- Descendant of a rare line of magical purple dragons
- Always the first Skylander to leap into action!

FROZEN THOUGHTS

During his frozen years, Spyro tells me he spent much of his time planning how to lead his fellow Skylanders home. I suspect breathing fire at a certain bald-headed über-villain also crossed his mind.

90%

MAGIC RATING

16

DOUBLE TROUBLE

FACTFILE

- Great caster of ancient spells
- Generally, a bit of a loner
- Has a life-long obsession with magic
- Loves exploring (never, ever call it 'shopping') for new spell ingredients.

MAGIC RATING

82%

FROZEN THOUGHTS

There are three things that would have been running through Double Trouble's mind during his frozen state: Magic, Magic and Magic!

That's right! This masked, magical guru has spent so long thinking about the subject that he's hardly ever made a friend in his life. Aww!

WRECKING BALL

FACTFILE

- This crazy Skylander started life as a simple grub worm
- Has a giant appetite - so that tongue sure comes in handy!
- Reminds Eon of a favourite childhood pet
- Eon named him Wrecking Ball after he destroyed some statues . . . by wrecking them!

FROZEN THOUGHTS

Being a frozen statue was a living nightmare for Wrecking Ball. This lively, giant blue grub worm is never content unless he's smashing the place up (never on purpose he would add). His thoughts would have been split between food and how to unleash his rapidly building energy.

74%

MAGIC RATING

VOODOOD

FACTFILE

- Was part of the revered Ooga Warrior tribe
- Discovered the Axe Reaver in the Cave of Trials
- Became a leader amongst the warriors
- After facing the Darkness, Voodood returned – the last of his tribe

MAGIC RATING

⬦⬦⬦⬦⬦⬦⬦⬦⬦⬦ 66%

FROZEN THOUGHTS

Voodood has had many adventures, and his time frozen in space was a time of reflection. He lost many fellow tribe members when they first confronted the Darkness. Although this made him emotionally stronger, he will never forget his greatest friends – or that crazy-eyed villain who banished them.

SECRETS OF THE ELEMENTS:
MAGIC

As you'll probably have noticed, Magic is the most powerful element in Skylands. Throughout time there have been those who have used it for good, but also those who have sought to harness its powers for . . . well, bad.

ARKEYAN MAGIC SECRETS

One group who definitely fall into the second category are the Ancient Arkeyans. Many moons ago, they ruled Skylands with an iron fist (which tends to hurt!). They loved a good secret . . . which, sadly, means there is much that even I don't know about them! If there's one thing I hate, it's secrets.

KAOS THEORY

I don't need to tell you who the latest person is to harness Magic for his own evil bidding - Kaos of course! As much as I'd like to ridicule him there is no doubt that he is definitely powerful and knows how to work dark Magic - as his destruction of the Core of Light proved.

THE MANY FACES OF KAOS (WELL, TWO ACTUALLY!)

THE ELDER ELEMENTALS

EON LOOKS SKYWARD FOR MAGICAL INSPIRATION.

It is believed that many of the core secrets of Magic were learned and developed by the Elder Elementals. They were the most powerful beings to have ever lived. Unfortunately, no one has seen an Elder Elemental in centuries, so it's difficult to ask them any questions!

CALI'S HEROIC CHALLENGES

At last – here's a section dedicated to my gal; my Cali! Let me tell you a thing or three about the Heroic Challenges she sets the Skylanders. After all, there's nobody better at hero training than Cali! Well, except me of course.

JUMP FOR IT!

This tale had me bouncing! Oh, I'm good! Cali challenged Wrecking Ball to collect as many Magic charms as he could, using jump pads to bounce from one to the next. Well, that crazy, far-out grub worm was like me in the balloon cockpit – pretty reckless! He was outta control but when the time was up not only had he collected all the Magic charms, but he'd also broken the Skylanders record for most bounces on a jump pad ever! Nice one, small Magic blue guy.

SPELL PUNKED!

This looks like a challenge for Voodood - and it is! My Cali sent The 'Dood to a beautiful, sunshiney island to bring back an ancient book of Magic. Sounds like a stroll, right? But this was no romantic vacation (which is a good job, as I'd get way jealous!). You see, when he arrived, he found the place was crawling with spell punks! One from each element, if you wanna get technical. So it was time for Voodood to swing his Axe Reaver all over the place and do some serious punking.

YOU DO NOT WANT TO BE ON THE SPELL PUNKS' SIDE WHEN VOODOOD GETS MAD!

MAGIC
TO THE CORE

FLYNN'S FABLES

Every Skylander loves a heroic challenge, right? Well this competitive edge lead Spyro and Trigger Happy to a competition that was nearly Spyro's undoing. Check it out!

As we all know, Trigger Happy is a kinda hypo guy, so one day he came up with an idea to liven up his day. He set Spyro a challenge. He bet that he could fire his gold coins higher than Spyro could fly.

'No way!' said Spyro. Well, I guess that's what he said as I wasn't there!

So, the challenge began. Spyro launched into the sky faster than my hot air balloon. He swooped into the air like . . . well . . . a swooping purple dragon whatsa-me-bob!

Trigger Happy blasted his coins into the abyss and Spyro

soared even higher to beat them.

Now, no-one really knows what happens next. Trigger Happy would tell ya that Kaos blasted Spyro from the sky. Spyro would say that Trigger Happy shot him! Anyway, Spyro's left wing suddenly went totally numb and he plummeted towards the ground like a heavy plummeting thing.

Spyro is one smart cookie though and caught a glimpse of the Core of Light in the distance. He swooped towards it with all his dragony strength, knowing it was his only chance. Just in time, he flew into the beam of light that quickly pulled him down to the ground. When Spyro rolled clear of the light his wing was tingling (the same way my heart does when I think of Cali! Oh, Cali!) Anyway, when he stood up his wing was healed.

The only explanation seems to be that he must have harnessed the Magic element from the Core of Light to save himself. To this day we still don't know if Trigger Happy or Kaos was to blame, but let's just say that no one else saw Kaos in Skylands on that particular day! Ouch!

ELEMENTAL GATES: MAGIC LOCATIONS

The Magic Element is extremely strong across all of Skylands. By analysing the data that has been compiled from maps and ancient scrolls, we can see that there are many Magic Element gates littered across our world. Here are some we have discovered . . .

SHATTERED ISLAND

We have learned that there is a Magic Element gate here that leads to a place called Turtle Hideout.

ACCESS OF LOCATION

HARD

EASY

DARK WATER COVE

This land holds a Magic Element gate to Lost Rigger's Cove. This area is particularly strong with the Magic Element. Beware of stepping through this gate though, as you are likely to encounter the Squidface Brute. Nasty!

ACCESS OF LOCATION

HARD

EASY

TREETOP TERRACE

This gate is well protected. Drow Spearmen and a Life Spell Punk will try to prohibit your entry. Defeat them to gain access to this elemental gate.

ACCESS OF LOCATION

HARD

EASY

LAIR OF KAOS

Kaos' dark fortress appears to hold the final Magic Elemental gate. Be warned – this is not a safe place to enter. Once inside the castle, the Path of Fangs is especially strong in the Magic Element. Reaching the end of this perilous path will reveal the final Magic Element gate.

ACCESS OF LOCATION

EASY

HARD

BURNING TROUBLE

FLYNN'S FABLES

So, you already know all about Double Trouble's expedition to find a rare Whispering Water Lily that ended up creating clones of the lively spellcaster. But I bet you haven't heard this little tale of how he played a trick on Eruptor. It was so funny that Eruptor was left smoking with rage!

It started when Eruptor was trying to think of ways to make himself even stronger and more powerful. It was then that he saw Double Trouble doing some training with his micro doubles and this gave Eruptor an idea. 'If only I had a load of micro doubles,' he thought. 'That could quadruplify my fiery powerness and make me almost unstoppable!'

So, Eruptor asked Double Trouble if the same spell could be cast on him and what he had to do to make the magic work . . . and his very own micro

doubles appear.

Sensing an opportunity for some fun, Double Trouble had a look around. He saw a sunflower next to the path and his crazy brain got to work. He told Eruptor that he could perform the spell, but for the magic to work, he would have to wear a Singing Sunflower . . . for the entire day.

Eruptor was so keen to get his own micro Eruptors, that he slapped it right in the middle of his forehead.

That night Eruptor returned, with the now slightly singed flower still perched a-top his fiery head. 'This better have been worth it!' he cried.

'Oh, it was!' replied Double

Trouble. 'Seeing you wearing that flower all day was the funniest thing I've seen in ages!' Sweet!

Double Trouble got out of there double fast, as the hot-headed lava guy erupted into a fiery rage!

And what happened to Double Trouble? Well, he kept a low profile for quite some time.

OOGA WARRIORS: THE MAGIC ARMY

The Ooga Warriors were one of the most revered tribes in all of Skylands. They were focused and deadly, and yet something haunted them. Every night wild dragons circled overhead forcing the Oogas to remain sheltered until daybreak. Those who had not heeded these warnings were often lost and presumed eaten!

The only thing that was known to destroy these dragons was the Axe Reaver. This was an ancient and magical axe that had been lost for centuries. Legend says that the axe grows stronger in power if wielded by a warrior who possesses true inner magic. If this was proven to be true, then whoever swung it was enriched with mystical powers of combat beyond their wildest dreams.

The legendary axe remained lost until Voodood rediscovered it in the Cave of Trials as a young warrior. With the Axe Reaver in his hands, Voodood became the leader of the tribe.

THE OOGA WARRIORS AND THE DRAGONS HAD LONG-RUNNING BATTLE

THE OOGA'S GREAT WAR

Voodood led his warriors through the most ferocious war his people had known. It was a war that lasted 100 nights, but strangely only thirty-seven days, and it saw thousands of beasts descend upon their tribe. The Oogas boasted many great and powerful warriors, all of whom played their part in defeating the enemy – and yet, one played a greater role. With the Axe Reaver, Voodood managed to slay three times as many beasts as his fellow tribesmen. The legend of the story says that the axe almost had a life of its own – a magical power that extended beyond Voodood's hands and brought the meanest and most ferocious beasts that Skylands has ever seen to their knees!

VOODOOD TURNED THE WAR.

MINE
DESTRUCTION

FLYNN'S
FABLES

In all the time I've known Wrecking Ball he's never got bored . . . as long as he's got plenty of things to smash up, that is! Yep! That's right. This crazy blue grub worm just loves to smash things. This often gets him into quite a bit of trouble around Skylands, but his wild behaviour was nearly the end of him on one particular occasion.

The Wreckmeister was rolling across Skylands as always, crushing the grass, flowers, bushes, trees and occasional Mabu who happened to get in his way. (Don't worry, no Mabu were hurt in the telling of this story). Before long he stopped and realized he had no idea where he was. He sat in the middle of the field with nothing left to destroy . . . and then something caught his eye. In the distance he saw an entrance to a mine. Sensing the opportunity for destruction, he rolled towards it and went

deeper and deeper into the depths of the mine until he stumbled across some of the biggest rocks he had ever seen.

'Wreck-n-Roll!' cried Wrecking Ball, and off he went. A smash here, a crash there, and a crunch and a bang (along with a noise I don't even know how to spell)! That little guy started destroying everything in sight. That is until he came across some mine dwellers who were less than happy to see what he was up to.

You guessed it! It was the Rocker Walkers. A humongous chamber full of them! He thought quickly about taking the whole lot of them on, but thought even more quickly that it was time to get out of there!

He rolled back up and out of the mine faster than a small, blue-tongued rolly thing and sprinted back to the other Skylanders as quickly as his little legs would carry him. A narrow escape, Wrecks!

The Darkness? Oh, that is spooky stuff alright. Of course, given that there are zombies in Skylands, and dragons, and probably zombie-dragons, few of us here are easily spooked. But the evil Darkness . . . well, this is GENUINELY hide-behind-your-couch-with-a-pillow-on-your-head kind of stuff. Maybe double pillows.

THE DARKNESS CASTING A SPOOKY GLOOM OVER SKYLANDS.

The Darkness has been an ever-present threat for Skylanders. I should know. There's nothing scarier than taking to the sky in my balloon and seeing those far-off dark clouds drifting closer. Hey! I know what you're thinking. Flynn's a great pilot right? Yeah, sure! But not even my great skills of balloon-maneuverability can out-fly the Darkness.

You see, the Darkness has this uncanny ability to take something good and make it bad. It's the ultimate evil force, but it can be harnessed. Shame that screwball Kaos is harnessing it for bad!

KAOS GOES CRAZY FOR DESTRUCTION

WHO IS DARK SPYRO?

No prizes for guessing that Dark Spyro is like regular Spyro . . . but darker! As we know, although Spyro is strong in the Magic element he also has an extraordinary ability with other Elemental powers, too. This can leave him open to the dangers of dark Magic. Creepy stuff!

Master Eon discovered this for the first time when the Darkness tried to enter Skylands and corrupt the Core of Light.

Being near such dark power, Spyro began to react in a way that no-one had ever seen before. His colours began to change as if he was absorbing a tremendous amount of dark Magic. Poor Master Eon was sent into a panic (not something we witness very often!). The great Portal Master had to think quickly and use his Magic to cast out the Darkness from within the purple dragon - but it was not gone forever.

DARK MAGIC UNLEASHED

Over the years, Spyro has learned to master his ability and absorb dark Magic more easily. Master Eon is very proud that he has learned to combine it with his existing powers to unleash even more devastating attacks against those who threaten Skylands. It is when this combination occurs that he transforms into Dark Spyro!

SECRET TO COMBINING MAGIC

Although he can wield incredible power when he becomes Dark Spyro, he also runs the risk of being consumed by darkness. The key factor in keeping the dark Magic at bay is Spyro's bravery - something I know very little about!

VOODOOD AND THE TREASURE CHEST

VOODOOD

It was a wonderful and glorious day in Skylands. Of course it was – I live there! Have I mentioned that everyone there loves me? Hey, I do what I can to make the people happy! Anyway, enough about me; this tale is about a treasure chest, Stealth Elf and my man Voodood.

Something unusual had happened that morning. A mysterious treasure chest had appeared on the water's edge and no one knew anything about it.

Voodood was the first to discover it but with no keys, he had no way of getting the thing open. He dragged the chest inland until he found Gill Grunt who, being a Gillman, knew more about the sea than any other Skylander. But even the wise Gillman had no idea how or why this chest would suddenly appear from the sea. So, he joined Voodood in trying to get it open. 'Stand back!' he cried as he

took aim with his harpoon. The harpoon flew chest-ward and jammed in one of the keyholes – but didn't open the chest. They both realised that to open such a chest might call for a weapon far more magical than Gill Grunt's harpoon, so they gave up! The End. Not really, just kidding! Of course, Voodood stepped forward with his legendary Axe Reaver. He swung the axe over his skull-covered head and thrust it down on the chest with more power than a large, heavy thrusty thing!

Then, ka-boom! The chest split in two to reveal a brilliant gemstone that Voodood recognised immediately. It was the remains of the gemstone in which he found the Axe Reaver. Voodood took the stone to Master Eon where he knew it could be put to good use in defending Skylands from evil. My hero!

MAGIC:
ELEMENTS UNITE

Magic is the most essential of all the eight Elements. It flows through everything and every other Element would be rendered almost powerless without its presence.

WEAKNESS

The Magic and Tech Elements are so strongly aligned that Magic Skylanders find their powers weakened in the presence of Tech Skylanders.

HOW MAGIC ENTWINES WITH THE OTHER ELEMENTS

AIR
Generates extra wind power

EARTH
Enchants the soil and Earth even more

FIRE
Fuels and intensifies the flames

LIFE
Enhances all living creatures

TECH
Strengthens crazy contraptions

UNDEAD
Enchants restless souls with dark Magic

WATER
Enriches Water's natural power

MAGIC
SKYLANDERS

VOODOOD

DOUBLE TROUBLE

SPYRO

WRECKING BALL

TECH
SKYLANDERS

BOOMER

DRILL SERGEANT

DROBOT

TRIGGER HAPPY

WHERE DOES TECH COME FROM?

Although Tech was around long before the Arkeyans existed 10,000 years ago, it was this ancient civilisation who perfected the use of technical machinery beyond any other. The proof of this can be discovered in the Arkeyan Armory. There lie some of the most powerful machines that have ever existed and all use Tech and Magic to function.

The Arkeyans spent thousands of years honing their technical skills, coming up with everything from terrifying weapons of war to new-fangled ways of quickly cooking their lunch (well, we all have to eat!). Their mighty machines have never been bettered, proving beyond all doubt that they were the ultimate Tech masterminds. Those clever clogs!

THERE'S NO MISTAKING THE ARKEYAN WAR MACHINES.

THE WAR MACHINES EVEN HAD THE ABILITY TO MOVE THROUGH MOLTEN LAVA!

THE GOLDEN GEAR AND GREEN PRIMORDIAL GOO

The Golden Gear lies at the heart of the entire universe. It is the intricate clockwork of the world. The Golden Gear drives everything that is Tech, but can only function when oiled with green primordial goo. There's an annoying, bald villain whom many would like to cover in green goo, too!

THE GOLDEN COGS THAT APPEAR IN THE CORE OF LIGHT.

DROBOT FIRES HIGH VELOCITY COGS FROM HIS ROBOTIC ARMOUR.

KAOS WITH THE GREEN GOO IN HIS POSSESSION.

47

GOLDEN AGE OF TECH

The Golden Gear is the very essence of Tech power in Skylands and, like the other Elemental sources, dates back hundreds of thousands of years. It is surprising, therefore, that it took a civilisation so long to harness it. The Eternal

THE ARKEYAN WAR MACHINES ARE UNLIKE ANY OTHERS CREATED BEFORE OR SINCE.

Elementals were aware of the Elemental sources, but were far too concerned with using their combined strength to create a device for banishing the Darkness. So, it fell to the Arkeyans to focus on Magic and Tech to realise its full potential in shaping our world. It's just as well they did, because they created some of the coolest war machines ever!

THE
DARKNESS STRIKES

SPREAD OF THE DARKNESS

Tech was the dominant force in Skylands for many years. Twinned with Magic, Tech became unstoppable during the Arkeyan rule and has dined out on that part of its history ever since! Even Kaos' total obliteration of the Core of Light is no match for Tech, especially when it gets together with its best pal, Magic.

TECH POWER!

TECH DESTROYED?

When Kaos tried to destroy the Skylanders, he sorely underestimated their resilience, especially those who were strong in Tech. Trigger Happy was part of the front line who retaliated against his attack. Although the Skylanders did all they could, they would not defeat the Darkness this time . . . much to Kaos' dastardly delight!

HAVE TECH, WILL TRAVEL

When the Tech Skylanders were propelled towards Earth, it was the beginning of their greatest adventure yet (not counting the time they spent frozen and not doing much, obviously).

TRIGGER HAPPY

TECH RATING

FACTFILE

- Nobody knows exactly where Trigger Happy came from
- Wild-eyed do-gooder with golden revolvers
- Travelled across Skylands ridding villages of bandits
- Always happy, always crazy, always lucky!

FROZEN THOUGHTS

Trigger Happy must have been one of the most frustrated Skylanders while in his frozen state. Always active, he can't keep still for a second. He'd probably have been thinking about getting back to Skylands as soon as he could to unleash those mighty golden guns!

DRILL SERGEANT

FACTFILE

- He lay dormant and deactivated for several millennia
- Eternally grateful to Terrafin for discovering him
- Uses Arkeyan armour and circuits to fight evil
- Makes a useful snowplough during the winter

FROZEN THOUGHTS

Drill Sergeant's first thought must have been, 'Oh no! Not again!'

After spending thousands of years with his 'off' button pressed and unable to move, being frozen in space must have been his worst nightmare. Just as those drills had begun to roll, like in the good old days, they were forced to cease once again.

TECH RATING

95%

BOOMER

FACTFILE

- Lifelong love of explosions
- Likes to make bombs, not war
- Skilled inventor
- Practises on unsuspecting sheep

TECH RATING

FROZEN THOUGHTS

Seeing the Core of Light destroyed would have been as hard for Boomer as any Skylander. Yet the explosion that followed must have been the best thing this pyrotechnic troll had ever seen. It's just a pity he was too busy being banished to have his camera ready!

DROBOT

FACTFILE

- The smartest dragon around (don't mention that to Spyro)
- Loves taking things apart to see how they work
- Assembled himself a powerful robotic suit
- His suit can fire spinning gears at high velocity

FROZEN THOUGHTS

Even his powerful, flight-enhanced robotic suit could do nothing to prevent him from joining the other Skylanders in frozen exile. He no doubt spent much of his time thinking up new gadgets to break the spell. So it's a bit of a pity he couldn't move to build them!

TECH RATING

SECRETS OF THE ELEMENTS:
TECH

The greatest secret of the Tech Element is its reliance on icky, sticky, primordial goo. It is the magic ingredient that transforms everyday, run-of-the-mill machines into all-singing, all-dancing mega-gadgets!

ARKEYAN TECH SECRETS

Just like my glasses, the secrets of Tech were lost for many years. From studying the Arkeyan Armory, we know that technology thrived in Skylands 10,000 years ago – but even the wisest Portal Masters couldn't find a way to operate the Arkeyans' massive war machines. If only the Arkeyans had left the instructions somewhere handy!

KAOS THEORY

If there's one person who would love to discover the secrets of Tech it is Kaos. He has turned his hand to Magic in harnessing the Darkness to do his evil bidding, but if he learned the secrets of Tech to build his own war machines then Skylands would become an even darker place than it is right now. Think of a cave with only one candle, and you get the idea!

CALI'S HEROIC CHALLENGES

When she's not thinking about me, Cali is putting the Skylanders through some pretty gruelling training. Of course, I could do this kinda thing in my sleep. That's why she never asks me to complete a challenge ... too easy!

Let's check some of them out ...

ENVIRONMENTALLY UNFRIENDLY

What is it with those Trolls and oil? It doesn't even taste good! Hey, I can think of at least three drinks that are way better. But for some reason they just can't get enough of it. Weird, huh? Anyway, when Cali heard they were stealing the stuff without a permit, she decided to make a Heroic Challenge out of it. That's my gal! So she sent Drill Sergeant along to bust up the Troll pipes (and the Trolls too, come to think of it), and he was only too happy to help.

OPERATION: SHEEP FREEDOM

You've probably noticed that sheep are everywhere in Skylands. I know Hugo has noticed, right Hugo?! But even Hugo would agree that locking the poor little guys up is way outta line. Sheep should be free to roam! When Cali heard that the Trolls had captured a bunch of them, she just had to step in. So she asked Boomer to wade right in there, put those Trolls straight and set the sheep free. You the man, Boom Box!

LEAD THOSE SHEEP TO FREEDOM! THEY'RE GETTING PECKISH.

FLYNN'S FABLES

READY, AIM, MIS-FIRE!

There were bolts of thunder around Skylands on this particular day. Or at least that's what we thought they were. Turns out it was Trigger Happy doing a spot of shooting practice. He'd drawn pictures of some evil bandits onto some rocks and was blasting them like there was no tomorrow.

Trigger Happy never misses! The trouble was that because he was shooting at rocks, his gold coin bullets kept ricocheting into the air and hitting anyone who was around. Luckily, the only things there were a few flocks of sheep, and they've got thick wool to soften the impact . . . so no harm done. Phew!

Anyway, shortly after a bit of target practice, Flameslinger came whizzing by. Trigger Happy didn't even know he was there until he was tapped on the shoulder . . . that's fast running!

My man Flame fancied a bit of a competition, but figured that shooting at a bunch of bandits drawn on rocks was child's play. He had a much better idea.

'See that blimp up there?' he said, pointing to the green air balloon that was passing overhead. 'Whoever can shoot over the top of that without hitting it is the ultimate champ.'

Trigger Happy had no problem with that . . . except that he likes to hit things when he shoots, so knew it would be a real challenge to miss it.

They both took aim.

'Only one shot each,' said Flameslinger. But Trigger Happy had his own plan.

Flameslinger shot one of his arrows high into the air and Trigger Happy unleashed a hail of bullets that sent any remaining sheep running for the hills.

Flameslinger's arrow arched perfectly over the top of the blimp as the cascade of golden bullets tore it into a million pieces.

It plummeted towards Skylands and was heading straight for my two buddies. Luckily, Master Eon caught sight of everything and a quick blast of Magic repaired the blimp and saved the day.

Master Eon was not happy, but Trigger Happy couldn't stop dancing around all day! As usual!

Tech is one of the oldest known Elements. Its source goes back tens of thousands of years, even way before the time of the Arkeyans. There are plenty of remnants relating to Tech scattered across our realm. Here are some that we know of . . .

PERILOUS PASTURES

Large areas of Perilous Pastures are extremely active in the Tech element, including Sunflower Ridge and a Tech Elemental Gate that leads to Bleating Highlands.

ACCESS OF LOCATION

EASY ⚙ ⚙ ⚙ ⚙ ⚙ HARD

TECH SKYLANDER TRIGGER HAPPY TEARS IT UP IN THE AREA KNOWN AS BLEATING HIGHLANDS.

CADAVEROUS CRYPT

ACCESS OF LOCATION

HARD

EASY

Not the most fun area of Skylands to visit, but Cadaverous Crypt is home to one of the few Tech Gates. If you can make it through the Catacombs and past the Rhu-Babies then you'll discover the area strongest in the Tech element – the Maze of Skulls.

MOLEKIN MINE

ACCESS OF LOCATION

HARD

EASY

The Molekin Mine is also a Tech haven. It's no wonder the Mabu who mine there need all the technical wisdom they can get to operate in those dark tunnels. Look out for the Tech gate that leads to The Secret Claim.

ARKEYAN ARMORY

ACCESS OF LOCATION

EASY

HARD

There is no area of Skylands where the Tech element is more powerful than the Arkeyan Armory. It's packed to the rafters with the most lavish war machines ever created. So it's surprising that no Tech Elemental Gate has ever been found down here . . . yet.

EXPLOSIVE MECHANIC

They don't come much more Techy than Drill Sergeant. He's been using his Arkeyan armour and circuits to fight evil and do good all across the realm. But when there's no evil to be fought, Drill Sergeant loves to get his Techy brain back in gear and do some repairing.

FLYNN'S FABLES

Gurglefin had a problem. He loved building things, but his latest machine just wasn't working.

'What I need is a Tech Skylander to help me,' he said. Just then, Drill Sergeant happened to roll past and decided to take a look at it. Pretty lucky, huh?

'I see the problem!' cried Drill Sergeant as he took a look inside the machine. 'Seems like there's a few cogs missing back here.'

He got to work banging and fixing the machine as only a Tech Skylander could. He started it up and rolled away as the

metal contraption roared into life, blasting a mass of fire and smoke up into the air.

Drill Sergeant was glad to help.

'What's this machine supposed to do anyway?' he asked.

Gurglefin could hardly contain his excitement. 'It's the power engine for my new awesome drilling machine!'

Well, as you can imagine, Drill Sergeant was less than pleased at the idea of a rival drill. But, as they say, if you can't beat 'em, join 'em – and that's exactly what he did.

He rolled to Master Eon, fetched some green primordial goo and helped Gurglefin invent one of the greatest drilling machines since the age of the Ancient Arkeyans.

Good job, D-Serg!

HUGO'S NOTES

WHO ARE THE TROLLS?

The Trolls are deeply unpleasant creatures (with the exception of Boomer of course!). They know their Tech, and are naturally calculating. Here's what we know about these small, green minions of Kaos.

THE TROLLS ARE ALWAYS OUT TO CAUSE TROUBLE!

RISE OF THE TROLLS

The Trolls were not always mere minions. Once, they lived under bridges collecting tolls from those who passed overhead. The fee was usually Fool's Gold (or Fool's Potatoes, for those who weren't quite foolish enough to be able to afford Fool's Gold).

One day, however, people stopped paying. So the poor old Trolls had to look elsewhere for work.

THE TROLLS AND KAOS

Kaos was quick to harness the technical minds of the Trolls in his quest to rule Skylands. The Trolls have taken over vast areas of Skylands on their master's behalf. On Oilspill Island, for example, they imprisoned the Gillmen and took over to drill for oil.

The Trolls also appear in Falling Forest, where they cut down all the trees in an attempt to find the Eternal Life Source. They also use their evil technical skills to battle against the Mabu Defense Force in Troll Warehouse.

The best way to offend trolls is to call them names - they're not the prettiest creatures in Skylands.

TROLLS LOVE THEIR WEAPONS OF DESTRUCTION!

TROLL FACTFILE

- Troll hobbies include war, conquest and an endless battle for world domination
- Violent, selfish and mean, they even refuse to be nice to their own mums
- They're great at making things - as long as those things are bombs
- Never, ever go on hoilday with them

TROLL TROUBLE

FLYNN'S FABLES

This is a little tale about Boomer and his Skylander pal, Gill Grunt. Brace yourself for an explosive story. Get it!?

The story goes that Boomer's day started off pretty well. He was feeling mighty pleased with himself, and why not? Gone were the days when he was forced to hang out with the Troll Army and wage pointless wars against tiny villages. Nowadays, Boomer rarely had to clap his bulging eyes on another troll. But that was all about to change.

Gill Grunt was out testing a few minor modifications to his power hose (he secretly hoped he could use it to carry float juice, his favourite drink). But the Gillman's day was ruined when a gang of trolls, out enjoying a spot of war-mongering, tried to nab his harpoon gun.

Gill leapt into action but, when he pulled the trigger on his juice-filled cannon, it jammed. Not cool! If only I'd been there to help. I could have helped out with the fight and still had time for breakfast. Ooo, breakfast . . . sounds good.

Thankfully, one guy who was there to help was Boomer. He launched his infamous sticks of dynamite straight towards the battle and BOOM! Or should I say SPLOSH! Sticky, fruity, extra-tangy float juice went everywhere, soaking the trolls

right through to their lumpy green skin. They were left with no choice but to scuttle off for that one thing all trolls hate: a bath.

Boomer had just saved the day and helped to keep the Tech secrets of Gill's harpoon hidden from the enemy. Hooray for the Boomy Man!

THE ARKEYAN LEGACY

The Ancient Arkeyans have forever left their mark on Skylands. Their incredible machines can still be found to this day, both above and below ground. So it's best to watch your step!

BUILDING SKYLANDS

A civilization as powerful as the Arkeyans could not rise and fall without leaving its mark. Almost everywhere you turn there are buildings, statues and monuments that, in some form, bear the hallmark of Arkeyan architecture. Take a look around and see for yourself! Just try not to climb on anything (it doesn't go down well with the locals).

AN ANCIENT ARKEYAN PLATFORM

CHOP CHOP: A LIVING (WELL, UNDEAD) REMNANT OF THE ARKEYAN ERA.

UNDERGROUND ARKEYANS

There is obviously no better place to experience the gadgets left behind by the Arkeyans than their very own Armory. Here you'll find everything from vast platforms to intricate doorways and consoles.

THE ARKEYANS JUST LOVED A GOOD CODE . . . WHICH IS PROBABLY WHY OPENING THEIR DOORS CAN BE SO TRICKY!

THE TECH COMPASS

Hey there! This is gonna be the last story in the book, so I thought I'd endulge myself by putting in one that features, yep, you guessed it . . . me! I don't come in until near the end, so try to be patient.

It had been a long time since Drobot had been back to the island where he discovered the ancient technology that formed his robotic suit. Every now and then he'd fly back there to see what he could find and to get some technical inspiration. On this particular occasion though, he headed back there for a purpose. His suit had a mini malfunction. The gears that shoot out of it had not been firing at their usual velocity for some time. Instead of blasting out super, mega fast they were more like standard, mega fast. . . or somewhere in between. Anyway, the mechanism basically needed a tweak, so Drobot headed back to the island to do some maintenance.

While he was there he searched around for new gadgets and stumbled across

balloon pilot I was (naturally) but that on the odd occasion my take-offs were less than perfect. Hey, I always mean to hit things as I take-off – how else will everyone know it's their last chance to see me? Anyway, Drobot thought that if I used it I'd be able to navigate a bit better. So, I took the Tech compass and boarded the balloon. The wind was strong and the balloon was ready to fly. I held the compass in my hands, read the data, launched the balloon, jerked into the air. . . and kinda dropped the compass. Yep! It plummeted away from Skylands faster than a falling boulder. Nice thought Drobot… but my flying is so good I guess I didn't really need it anyway!

something highly unusual. It was a silver Tech compass (this is where I come in!) The Tech compass was created to assist pilots with take-off and landing by analysing the surrounding area and feeding back vital stats (or some other crazy Tech nonsense).

So, Drobot brought the Tech compass back and gave it to me. He said he knew what a great

DROBOT'S INVENTIONS

Drobot is one of the smartest dragons ever. He's a gadget guru! Here, we take a look at the wowsie robotic suit he created while on a mysterious gadget-strewn island . . .

FLIGHT ENHANCEMENT TECHNOLOGY

Drobot is not the strongest flyer, but that turned out to be a blessing as it's what got him thinking about ways to enhance his flight performance. He found the answer in some unique technology that allowed him to become faster and more powerful than any other dragon alive!

SPINNING GEAR WEAPONRY

This is the second part of Drobot's attack. If he chooses not to use his laser beams he'll fire high velocity flying gears.

VOCAL SYNTHESIZER

His vocal synthesizer gives him a deep, booming voice.
I think Flynn believes it was modelled on him! Maybe if I had
a deeper voice people would take me more seriously. Oh well.

LASER BEAMS

The first line of Drobot's defences are the laser beams that he shoots from his peepers.

This form of attack brings a whole new meaning to the phrase, 'looks can kill!' Ouch!

TECH:
ELEMENTS UNITE

There's no power like Tech power! As the Arkeyans discovered, when Tech is combined with the other Elements it has the power to dominate the entire realm.

WEAKNESS

Tech Skylanders find themselves weakened against Earth Skylanders, but they are strengthened when opposed by Magic Elements.

HOW TECH ENTWINES WITH THE OTHER ELEMENTS

AIR
Empowers the might of the wind

EARTH
Churns the soil and earth into a frenzy

FIRE
Powers and ignites fire

LIFE
Super-equips all who can learn its strengths

MAGIC
Develops and powers inventions

UNDEAD
Arms even the un-deadliest soul

WATER
Turns placid lakes into river rapids

FAREWELL!

So, there ya go! No need to thank me, 'cause I already know how awesome I was at telling you everything you wanted to know. Don't mention it. Hey, if you wanna find out anything else then just keep an eye open for my air balloon. I don't plan on heading to Earth soon, but with my navigation who knows where I'll end up!

Thank you, new Portal Master, for taking the time to discover more about the Magic and Tech Elements. I trust this will aid you on your quest to help the Skylanders defeat Kaos. Hopefully, Flynn's ramblings didn't put you off. Once he gets started there's no stopping him and his tall tales!

Anyway, until next time . . . goodbye and good luck!

SKYLANDERS: TAKING THE BATTLE TO KAOS!